An Ear Is

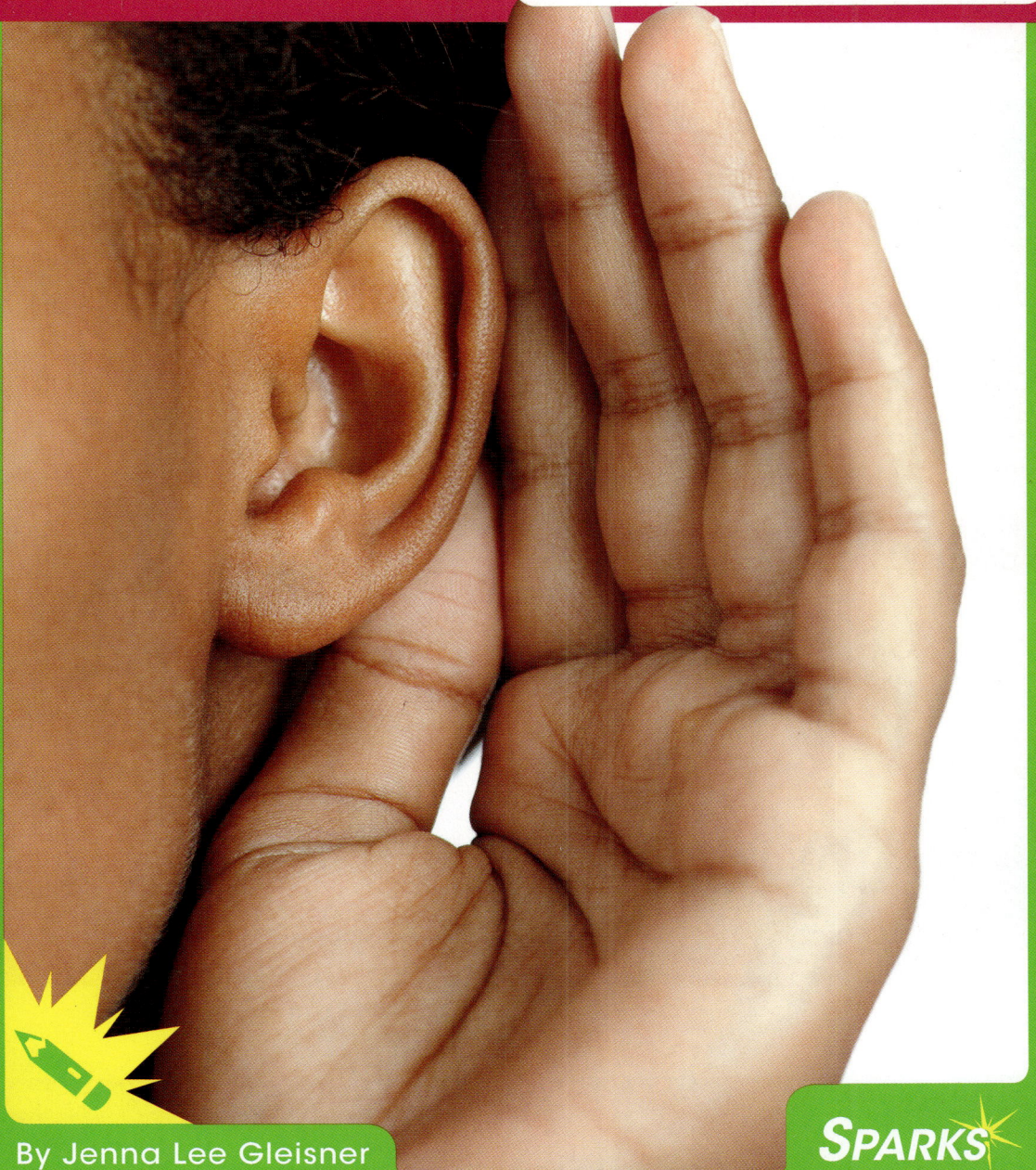

By Jenna Lee Gleisner

SPARKS

Picture Glossary

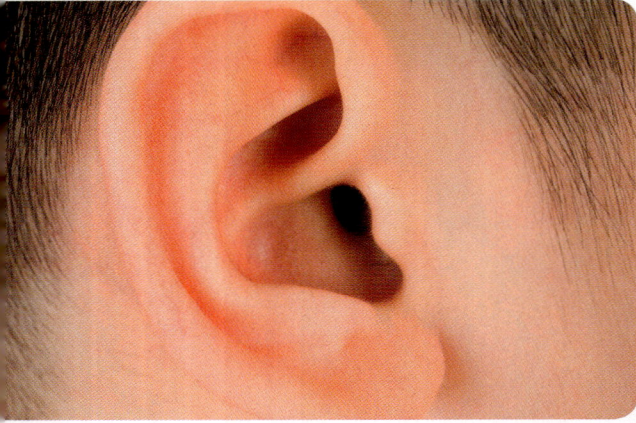

ear   4

hear   8

This is an ear.

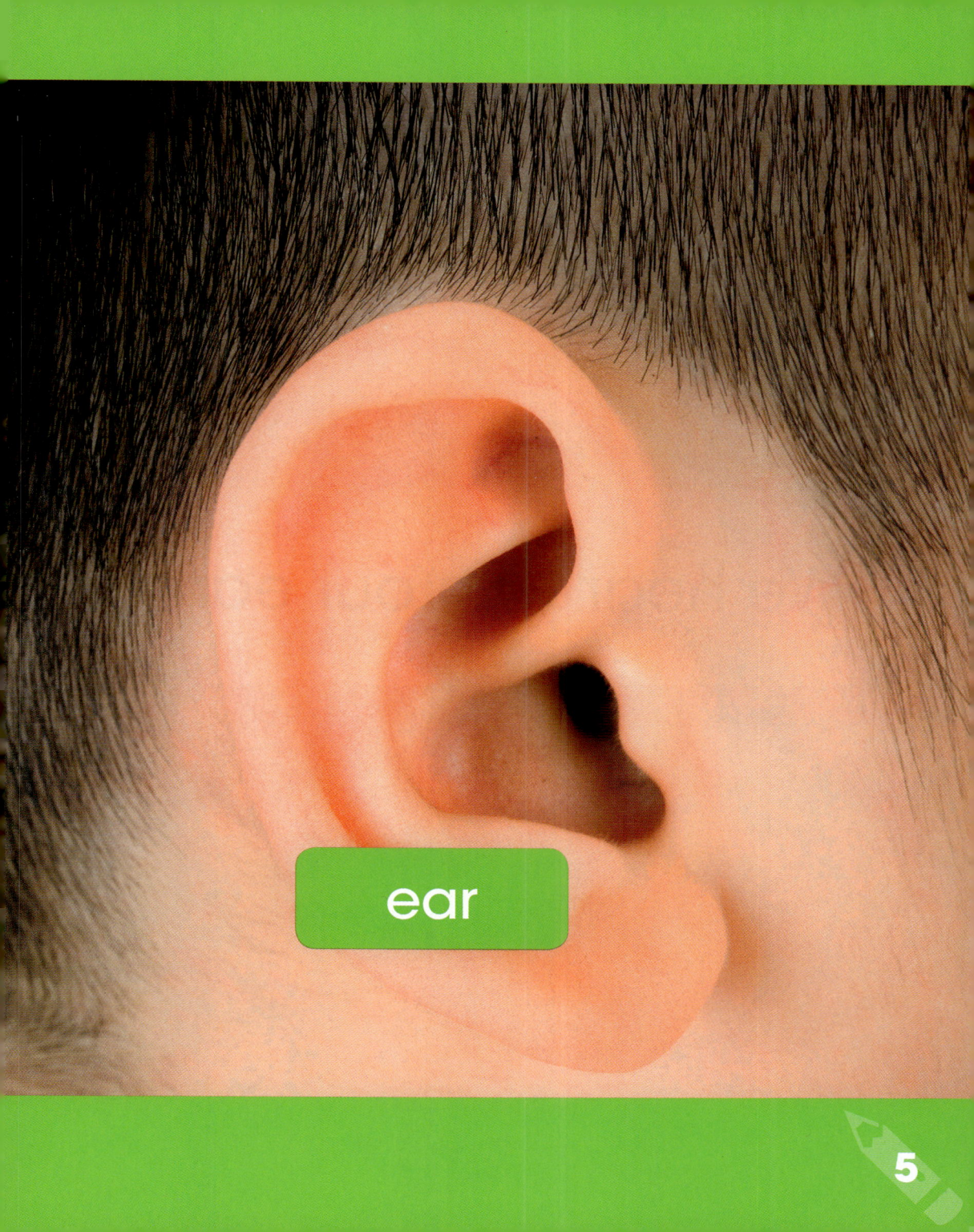

ear

We hear with our ears.

The boy can hear music with his ears.

hear

The girl is near her friend.

Her friend can hear her.

near

11

The boy can hear his father.

father

They are near the teacher.

They can hear the story.

story

Do You Know?

What does he hear with his ears?

music

friend

father

story